This book belongs to:

Unstoppable

. . . .

OXFORD
UNIVERSITY PRESS

Great Clarendon Street, Oxford OX2 6DP

Oxford University Press is a department of the University of Oxford.
It furthers the University's objective of excellence in research, scholarship,
and education by publishing worldwide in

Oxford New York

Auckland Cape Town Dar es Salaam Hong Kong Karachi
Kuala Lumpur Madrid Melbourne Mexico City Nairobi
New Delhi Shanghai Taipei Toronto

With offices in
Argentina Austria Brazil Chile Czech Republic France Greece
Guatemala Hungary Italy Japan Poland Portugal Singapore
South Korea Switzerland Thailand Turkey Ukraine Vietnam

British Library Cataloguing in Publication Data available

ISBN: 978-0-19-274410-4 (paperback)

10 9 8 7 6 5 4 3 2 1

Printed in China

Paper used in the production of this book is a natural, recyclable product made
from wood grown in sustainable forests. The manufacturing process conforms
to the environmental regulations of the country of origin

Dedicated to:

My fabulous Lawrence
+

Many thanks to the
Unstoppable A-team
Helen, Kate and Suzie

J.P

* * *

Unstoppable Max

Julia Patton

OXFORD
UNIVERSITY PRESS

Mummy peeked around the door.
'Almost bedtime, Max,' she said.
'So if you can tidy away your toys,
get into your clean pyjamas,
and feed Fluffy, I'll be back in five minutes.'

But Max didn't have any toys ...

he had an **army!**

And right now Major
Unstoppable Max

was in charge of
Operation Castle Attack

and he really
didn't want
to stop.

It was time to put on his thinking hat
and have a really good think.

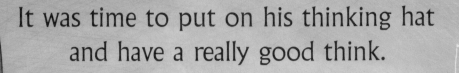

Thinking Hat

What **do you think**
Max should do?

Should he do something **sensible** like tidying up?

Should he do something **naughty** like keeping Mummy out of his bedroom?

South Pole

Should he do something **crazy** like going on an expedition to the South Pole?

Major Unstoppable Max had the answer.
He hid his army under the bed!
The mission was successful . . .

apart from a little paint-related incident.
Max was ready for Operation Clean Pyjamas.

But were the
clean pyjamas . . .

ready for Max?

It was time to put on his thinking hat
and have a really good think.

Thinking Hat

What **do you think**
Max should do?

Should he do something
sensible
like washing his hands
in the bathroom?

Should he do something
naughty
like washing his hands
in Fluffy's bowl?

Soap

Fish Food

Should he do something
crazy
like learning to play the tuba?

Major Unstoppable Max had the answer.
It was daring. It needed careful planning.
It was Mission Find New Pyjamas!

Ta-da!

Max was ready for his final challenge. Feeding Fluffy.

Fish Food

Everything went
exactly to plan.
Apart from a
small hole-related
incident.

It was time to put on his thinking hat
and have a really good think.

Thinking Hat

What do you think Max should do?

Should he do something
sensible
like asking Mummy
to help him?

Should he do something
naughty
like giving Fluffy a
strawberry sizzler instead?

Should he do something
crazy
like adopting an alligator?

Max

Major
Unstoppable Max
had the answer.

He needed his
thinking hat.
And some tape.
And he had to be
unstoppably quick.

Phew!
Max fed Fluffy just in time.

'All tidy and almost ready
for bed!' said Mummy.
'You **are** a good boy. Now,
pop to the bathroom and
brush your teeth.'

But Max didn't go to the bathroom ...

he went to his
secret laboratory!

And right now Professor Unstoppable Max
was inventing a Double Bubble Potion
and he really **didn't want** to stop.

A note for grown-ups

Oxford Owl is a FREE and easy-to-use website packed with support and advice about everything to do with reading.

Informative videos

Hints, tips and fun activities

Julia Donaldson's top tips for reading with your child

Help with choosing picture books

For this expert advice and much, much more about how children learn to read and how to keep them reading ...

LOOK
for Oxford Owl
www.oxfordowl.co.uk